Doctor Tilly

Originated by Polly Dunbar

WALKER
ENTERTAINMENT

Tilly and her friends were
having a great time
playing tag.

"You're it, Tilly!"

"Tilly's it,
watch out!"

"I'm coming
to get you!"

"Yipee!"

"Oh!"

Whoops! Hector tripped over a toy and landed – bump! – on the floor!

"Ow!"

Tilly rushed over.
"Oh, dear! Poor Hector!"

Tilly wiped Hector's tears and gave him a sip of water.

"There. All better," she said.

"You make a very good doctor," said Tumpty.

When Tumpty knocked his blocks over
he called out "Help!"
Doctor Tilly came to the rescue!

"Doctor Tilly will make you all better!" she said, wrapping him in bandages.

"But Tilly, I feel Ok..." said Tumpty.

"Well, I DID feel Ok."

Then Pru cried for help
because her car had broken down.

Doctor Tilly covered her in plasters.
"It's total bed-rest for you!"
she said.

"But ...

but ...

but ..."

squawked Pru,

"I'm fine!"

But when Tumpty came out in green spots,
Tilly didn't know what they were
or how to make them go away.

"This is terrible, I've tried everything!"
she said.

"But Tilly, I feel fine,"
said Tumpty.

Tilly felt sad.
"Maybe I'm not a good doctor
after all."

Tilly sat on the Huff Tuffet.
"Are you all right?" asked Pru.

"How are you feeling?" asked Hector.
"Thank you for asking," said Tilly. "Oh..."
Tilly realized she had never
asked her friends how *they* felt.

"How do we feel, everyone?"

"I'm glad you're all feeling fine," said Tilly.

"A good doctor should always listen to her patients," said Tilly.

"ACHOO! oh dear!"

"Are you all right, Tilly?" asked Tumpty.

Tilly didn't feel
well at all.

"Don't worry", Hector said,
"we'll make you better."

First published 2014 by Walker Entertainment
An imprint of Walker Books Ltd
87 Vauxhall Walk, London SE11 5HJ

2 4 6 8 10 9 7 5 3 1

© 2012 JAM Media and Walker Productions
Based on the animated series TILLY AND FRIENDS, developed and produced by Walker Productions and JAM Media
from the Walker Books 'Tilly and Friends' by Polly Dunbar. Licensed by Walker Productions Ltd.

This book has been typeset in Gill Sans and Boopee.

Printed in China

British Library Cataloguing in Publication Data:
a catalogue record for this book is available from the British Library

ISBN 978-1-4063-5724-0

www.walker.co.uk

See you again soon!